Pig's Big Feelings

Inquiries: kellybourne.ca/contact

ISBN: 978-1-7773896-0-4

First paperback edition March 2021

PIG'S BIG FEELINGS

Written by
Kelly Bourne

Illustrated by
Aparna Varma

Hello, my name's **Pig**!

I'm mostly quite happy.

Though sometimes I'm GRUMPY,
CRANKY, or SNAPPY.

I feel many feelings,
some **big** and some small.

Warm fuzzies,
cold pricklies —
I've had them
all.

Sometimes they're tricky
and swirl in my brain,
but I'll try my best to
describe and explain.

Although close, the word HAPPY
isn't quite right
for the carefree contentment
of flying my kite.

And SAD is okay,
but it's still not the best,
for losing my bike
and the lump in my chest.

I'm DEVASTATED

Being clear is important!
It lets people know
just what you're feeling,
your highs and your lows.

The secret, you ask,
to express all the goodness,
as well as the bumps
and the lumps
of life's fullness?

It's **naming your feelings**
and building a list
of words to describe
all your wonder and bliss.

Come here my dear friend,
and I'll show you the way.
Let's name all your feelings,
no need to delay!

JOY is the word I would
choose in the case
when Mom pulls me close
for a snuggly embrace.

I'm DELIGHTED! ECSTATIC!

On hot summer days,
playing with friends
beneath the sun's rays.

The magical squish
of fresh mud on my feet!

Slipping and sliding

makes me feel complete.

But everyone knows
life is more than just hugs,

and sometimes we're
SCARED,

or
ANXIOUS,

or

UGH!!!

Like that time Aunt Bernice
thought it would be a ball
to toss 'round the pigskin
with family last fall.

"Aunt Bernice!" I cried, feeling quite **HORRIFIED**,

"That football you're holding was once Uncle Clyde!"

CLYDE

Or like that time
that I tried and I tried
to prove everyone wrong
and take high to the sky.

They laughed and they sneered —
making jokes, poking fun!
I was EMBARRASSED,
FORLORN,
and completely UNDONE.

REJECTED and lost, yet I never did stray.

Then one day
I did it!

I flew up and
away!

Boy, was I PROUD!

I was so filled with glee!
Soaring through clouds
I felt PLAYFUL and FREE.

A parade was arranged
for my unlikely flight
when a wild motorcycle
clipped Shirley McNight.

The FURY! The ANGER!
But then the RELIEF,

of knowing my dear friend
would not be ground beef!

Despite being shaken
and feeling such FLUSTER

we made it in time
and found the big cluster.

The town was
EXCITED,
ELATED,
EUPHORIC!
To join in a party
that would be historic.

The first pig to fly!
It was such a big deal!

Being so NERVOUS

I let out a squeal.

Looking back at the feelings
I felt through the course
of reaching my goal
I must reinforce,

that whether you're ANGRY, or
ANXIOUS, or BORED,
accepting yourself is the
greatest reward.

Let this be a lesson
from one pig to you,
naming your feelings
will help you stay true.

They make you who you are
and there's no other way.

The **best** way to be
is **yourself** every day!

Pig's Guide to What Feelings Feel Like

Angry: When I'm angry my body gets hot and it feels like steam is about to come out of my ears. I feel angry when people are mean to my friends.

Bored: When I'm bored my head feels empty and I'm out of ideas. I feel bored when I have nothing to do.

Content: Being content feels peaceful. When I'm content my body is relaxed and I have everything I need. I feel content reading stories with my grandma.

Cranky: When I'm cranky the littlest things bug me. I feel cranky when I don't get a good night's sleep.

Devastated: When I'm devastated I want to cry and can't imagine things getting better. I feel devastated when I lose my favourite blankie.

Embarrassed: When I'm embarrassed my face feels hot and I want to hide. I feel embarrassed when I wear pajamas to school, but it's not pajama day.

Excited: When I'm excited it feels like there are fireflies dancing on my skin. I feel excited when it's time for my friend's birthday party.

Flustered: When I'm flustered my thoughts are jumbled and I can't think straight. I feel flustered when my teacher calls on me and I don't know the answer.

Furious: When I'm furious I feel like a volcano about to erupt. I feel furious when my sister breaks my new birthday present on purpose.

Grumpy: When I'm grumpy it feels like there is a black cloud following me. I feel grumpy when I'm tired and people won't stop asking me questions.

Horrified: Horrified is when I'm in shock about something gross or scary. I feel horrified when I watch my baby brother try to eat a worm.

Nervous: When I'm nervous it feels like there are a million butterflies in my tummy. I feel nervous when I need to make a speech in front of the class.

Relieved: I feel relieved when I can finally relax after being tense or on edge. I feel relieved when I find a toy I thought I'd lost.

Scared: When I'm scared my chest gets tight and my thoughts are blurry with worry. I feel scared when I have a bad dream.

What do these feelings feel like for you?
What other feelings can you pick out from the story?

Download the Discussion Guide at kellybourne.ca/pig

Kelly Bourne

Author

Growing up on a pig farm, Kelly's hobbies included sneaking piglets out of the barn and getting in trouble for reading past bedtime. Kelly grew up to be a pediatric nurse with a master's degree in counseling and now spends her time helping kids feel their feelings.
You can learn more about how Kelly helps families at kellybourne.ca

Aparna Varma

Illustrator

Aparna grew up in the bustling city of New Delhi, India and often got in trouble for drawing all over her homework. Aparna studied Animation and Film in University and currently works in TV Animation Production in Toronto.
You can find more of her work at aparnavarma.com

Made in the USA
Monee, IL
29 April 2021